CW00432503

BUSTIN' LOOSE

REAL ESTATE RESCUE COZY MYSTERIES, BOOK 9

PATTI BENNING

SUMMER PRESCOTT BOOKS PUBLISHING

CHAPTER ONE

A year ago, Flora Abner worked at a dreary job that she hated, with no end in sight. Today, she was working at a hardware store. It may not have sounded like an improvement if you had asked her a year ago, but she had never been happier.

"Thank you, and please come again. I hope you get the leak figured out!"

She waved as her most recent customer left the store, a genuine smile on her face. Becoming part-owner of a small-town hardware store had never been her plan, but she couldn't say she regretted it. There was something about *owning* the business that made her hours there feel a lot less dull than they might have otherwise.

It also helped that this was just her side gig. Her

main focus was on flipping the old farmhouse she had purchased and moved into the year before. Now that it was spring, and the weather was improving, she was preparing to tackle some of the larger outdoor projects she had been putting off. Namely, dredging and landscaping the small pond in the woods behind her house. Right now, it was a mess of branches, old leaves, and trash. She wanted to clean it up and cut some well-groomed walking paths through the trees. She needed to sell the house at a decent profit, and the multiple acres of land were going to be a big draw for any potential buyer.

"Excuse me, Ms. Abner?"

She forced her thoughts back to the present and turned to see the hardware store's new employee, Ellison Adams, trying to get her attention.

"Sorry, I was lost in thought. What's going on? Oh, and I told you, just call me Flora. Ms. Abner makes me feel old."

He gave a slight grimace. For some reason, it was hard for him to call herself and her business-partner-slash-boyfriend Grady Barnes by their given names. It *did* make her feel old. She and Grady were in their thirties, and Ellison was not quite twenty. Being called Ms. Abner made her feel like someone's mom.

Which was fine. Really. She would just rather be Flora.

"The woman I'm helping in the garden center needs five bags of gravel and we only have two. When are we getting more in?"

"I think the next shipment of gravel and mulch is supposed to come Friday," she said, ruffling through the papers on the front counter. She and Grady had slowly been upgrading to a new computer system, but the previous owner had kept all of his records by hand, and it wasn't an easy habit for Grady to break. "Yeah, it's Friday. If she wants to pay for them when she checks out today, we'll put them aside for her and she can pick them up over the weekend."

"I'll tell her," Ellison said. "Thanks!"

He hurried away to the back of the store, where the exit to the garden center was. Flora turned around and leaned back against the front counter, gazing out the window. The sky was overcast, and it had been drizzling all day. She waited for a few minutes, watching the occasional car drive past on Main Street, then turned back around and grabbed one of the notebooks on the counter, flipping it open to her to-do list. She needed to pick a few things up for the house while she was here. It wasn't just the pond that needed work

— she had finished most of the interior repairs that the house needed over the winter, but she still had to replace the kitchen counters and do a few smaller fixes here and there. She wanted to get matching hardware for the bathrooms today. The current fixtures were dated, and new towel rods, toilet paper holders, and vent register covers would help with first impressions.

She felt the same dull pain as she always did at the thought of selling the house, but did her best to ignore it. Part of flipping houses was selling them when the work was done. That was just a fact. She hadn't expected to fall in love with the house and the little Kentucky town of Warbler, was all. Between the money she owed and the fact that she needed more income than a part-ownership and part-time work at the hardware store could provide, there was no getting out of it. She had to sell the place in just under a year.

The bell over the front door jingled and she turned, her customer service smile morphing into something a lot warmer when she saw who had come into the store. The town and the house weren't all she had fallen in love with. Grady Barnes had been her first friend here in Warbler, and that relationship had quickly become something more. They had been dating ever since the previous summer. When she bought the hardware store with him, they had only been together for a few months. It had been a risk, both financially and emotionally, but she hadn't had a single reason to regret it. Having ownership in a hardware store had turned out to be a great investment for someone who wanted to flip houses for a living, and it had also brought her and Grady closer than ever. They worked well together, and she couldn't have asked for a better partner, both in the business and in the romantic sense of the word.

"Hey," she said. "Dreary afternoon, isn't it?"

"Everything is *damp*," he muttered, sounding displeased by the fact. Despite his ire at the weather, he greeted her with a gentle kiss, then looked around the mostly empty store. "Not our busiest day, I take it?"

"We've had a few customers, and Ellison's helping someone in the garden center right now, but it's been quiet. It's the sort of day where most people want to cozy up at home with a book, I guess."

"At least all this rain is giving us a chance to see if those roof repairs we made are holding up."

He eyed the ceiling suspiciously, but the interior of the store remained dry. Gone were the slow, steady drips that had sprung up over the winter. Flora was proud of the fact that she had gone up on the roof and helped him make the repairs herself. A year and a half ago, she had hardly known how to hold a hammer. Doing most of her own repairs on her house had paid off in bushels with practical knowledge and skills.

"If you're here for the afternoon, I might pick up what I need for the bathrooms at home and get going," she said. "I want to get them done, so I can focus on the kitchen once the new counter tops arrive next week."

"Go ahead," he said. "I'll be here until close. Sorry I'm later than usual. I got an… unexpected call just as I was about to leave my place."

She raised an eyebrow. "Unexpected in a good way or a bad way?"

He hesitated. "I'm not sure. It's from the prison. My brother got an early release. He's getting out this weekend."

Flora blinked. She knew Grady had a brother, and that said brother had a reputation around town as a troublemaker and was currently in prison on a drug-related charge, but she had never met the man and Grady rarely talked about him.

"His name's Wade, right?" she asked. Grady nodded. "Well, that's good. I'm sure he'll be glad to be out, at least."

"Yeah. He'll have to stay with me until he gets his feet under him." He didn't look thrilled at the prospect. "It'll be cramped, but I can't turn him away. He's family, you know?"

"I get it. If one of my siblings needed somewhere to stay, I'd offer them my spare room in a heartbeat."

Not that either of them would ever need it. She and Grady came from very different financial backgrounds. She was the black sheep of her family, having gone voluntarily from a comfortable, if mind-numbing, white-collar job to a career that demanded a lot more physical labor with much less guaranteed income. Grady, she knew, hadn't had much money for most of his life, though now that he was the majority owner of the hardware store, that was beginning to change.

"This probably means I'll have to cancel our date on Saturday," he told her. "I feel bad about it, but I need to go pick him up and help him get settled in. He doesn't have anyone else."

"Don't worry about it," she said, smiling. "Just focus on your brother. I'm happy to focus on the house and spend some time with Amaretto this weekend. I should probably have Beth over for tea at some point too. I've been so busy lately, I keep having to turn her down when she asks me to socialize."

Beth was her elderly neighbor, a kind of opinionated woman who had befriended Flora when she first moved in. She dropped by to chat whenever she saw Flora's truck in the driveway, and even though she drove Flora up the wall sometimes, she had come to value the older woman's friendship. She was kind-hearted and well-meaning, even if she could be a bit much sometimes.

"I'll make it up to you later," he promised. "Things should go back to normal after this weekend."

CHAPTER TWO

As the week went on, Flora could tell that Grady was nervous about his brother's homecoming. She wasn't sure how to feel about it either. She had never known someone who had been to *prison* before. Still, she did her best to pretend everything was normal, and when she arrived at the hardware store to take the afternoon shift that Saturday, she sent Grady off with an extra tight hug, and the hope that his brother got settled in over the weekend without any problems.

With the hardware store closed on Sundays, she had a much-needed day off the next day. She forced herself to take time off from working on the house, too. Going from an office job with set hours to a job where the only boss was herself and she could work anytime she was at the house had taken some getting used to, and she had learned the hard way that she *needed* to take at least one day completely off each week, no matter how tempting it was to do just one or two small jobs around the house.

Before she started working part-time at the hardware store, she took both Saturday and Sunday off most weeks. Hopefully, once Ellison was more confident with opening and closing the store, she could start doing that again soon. For now, he still needed someone else with him while he worked. Part of the reason was because she and Grady kept changing things. The store's previous owner, Mr. Brant, hadn't made a single change to the store for decades, and now the two of them were trying to figure out a good balance between modernizing the place, and keeping to the small-business feel the locals loved.

Sunday was a lazy day spent with her fluffy white Persian cat, Amaretto, a frozen pizza, and a few episodes of a show she was eager to catch up on. Grady didn't call, but she did get a text from him letting her know he was thinking of her. She was beyond happy that she had finally been able to convince the man to buy a cell phone. Previously, the only way to contact him had been to call his land line and hope he was home.

She felt refreshed and ready for another week

when Monday came around. Putting off making her own coffee in favor of a stop at Violet Delights, the local coffee shop, for some *good* coffee, she went through her morning routine, kissed the top of her cat's fluffy head goodbye, and hopped into her truck. She was eager to hear all about Wade's first weekend out of prison. It was just a matter of time before she met the man now that he was back in town, but she hoped he didn't tag along with Grady to the store. She wanted a chance to talk to him first, and hear about how his brother was faring.

Violet Delights had been one of the very first places Flora had gone back to when she moved to Warbler, and it was there that she had met her now-best-friend, the owner of the coffee shop, Violet. With her black hair, her purple contact lenses, and her stylish clothes, the other woman didn't look like she belonged in such a small Southern town, and the interior of the coffee shop was no different. Every single inch of the place was done up in various shades of purple. It was like stepping into another world whenever she visited. Flora loved the place — and not just because their white chocolate caramel latte was to die for.

There was a short line inside when she arrived. She waved at Violet from the back of it, then waited for her turn as her friend made drinks with ease Flora envied. She had spent a few days helping out at the coffee shop the year before, and hadn't progressed much beyond pouring drip coffee and cleaning the counters. It was *hard* to remember all of the recipes for the various drinks, though she supposed the fact that Violet had come up with all of them herself probably helped.

"Good morning," Violet chirped when Flora reached the front of the line. "Do you want your regular?"

"I'm boring like that," Flora said, grinning. "Busy morning?"

"Mondays always are," her friend said as she accepted Flora's card and ran it before handing it back. "I think it helps people get out of bed at the start of a new week when they know they can treat themselves a little on their way to work."

"I think they're on to something. Having a latte in my hand definitely makes it a little easier to open the hardware store."

"Doesn't Grady open most days?" Violet asked as she started making the drink.

"He usually opens five of the six days we're open," Flora said. "Mostly because he's a lot better at waking up early than I am. Hopefully Ellison will be able to take over some of those days once he's trained up a bit. I told him I'd handle opening today, though." She inched closer to the counter, lowering her voice. "His brother, Wade, got out of prison this weekend and is staying with him. I didn't want him to have to rush back to work first thing on Monday morning after being busy all weekend."

"Wade's out?" Violet's eyes widened slightly. "Wow. I almost forgot about him."

"Do you know him?" Flora asked. Violet was friends with Grady too, but Flora had never heard her mention his brother.

"Not exactly. It's more that I know *of* him. He's not a great guy. I know he's been arrested more than once, but this last one was the only one to stick. Grady's a good person, we both know that, but don't expect his brother to be anything like him."

"I don't," Flora said. "I haven't met him yet, and if I'm being honest, I'm a little nervous about it."

"I'm sure it will be fine," Violet said, giving her a reassuring smile as she handed the latte over. "Have a good day at work. Let me know if you want to do anything this evening. I should be able to get out of here at three."

"I should be able to leave the hardware store by then too. Maybe we can get lunch."

Cheered by the thought, she said a quick goodbye to her friend and left, not wanting to hold up the line.

She parked in the lot behind the hardware store and let herself in through the back door. It felt odd to admit it, but she loved the way the hardware store felt first thing in the morning, with the lights dimmed and completely silent except for the hum of the central air unit. It was peaceful. She had a few minutes to spare before she had to open the store, and she spent them walking the aisles, double checking that everything was in place and admiring the new shelving units Grady had installed. The old, wooden floors were still creaky, but the two of them had cleaned and polished the wood until it looked almost new. They had reorganized too, widening the aisles so it was easier for customers to maneuver the carts and moving the most commonly sought after items to the front.

They had also added a catalog of everything they could order but didn't usually keep in stock, along with a stack of order forms and a cup full of pens. While the steady trickle of customers they got each day was helpful and welcome, the bulk of their sales came from small-time contractors who needed supplies for their businesses. The catalog and order forms streamlined the process, so their biggest customers no longer had to call in to place sometimes lengthy or complicated orders. They could fill out a form in the store, or even take one home and drop it in the drop box whenever they had time.

Flora wanted to implement an online ordering system too, but that was a work in progress.

She spent an easy morning running the register and chatting with the handful of customers who stopped in. She was beginning to recognize the regulars. One of them, Teddy Martin, was a grizzled yet friendly man who ran a scrap metal business. He was fixing up his office, and she was ringing him up for a few pails of white paint when she spotted another customer striding toward the door with a new drill in a box under one arm.

Shoplifting was so rare that she almost didn't register what was happening. She glanced toward the man out of reflex, then turned her attention back to Teddy, opened her mouth to tell him the total, then paused and snapped her gaze back toward the man with the drill.

"Hey! You need to pay for that!"

The man froze. She saw his eyes move from the door, to her, then back again and knew he was going to make a run for it an instant before he started to move.

CHAPTER THREE

She took a hurried step toward him right as he broke
for the door. He yanked it open, making the bell jingle
violently, and rushed outside. She wavered in place,
not sure if she should pursue or not.

"I'll get him!" Teddy said. Before she could ask
him not to get involved, he took off after the thief.
Now Flora *had* to follow. She could hardly let a
customer get into a fight with a shoplifter on her
account.

She raced after them, through the store's door and
down the sidewalk. The thief didn't make it very far
— Teddy caught up with him less than halfway down
the block and grabbed the back of the man's shirt. He
spun around, still gripping the new drill. Flora
skidded to a stop a few feet away from them.

"I hate thieves," Teddy grumbled, tightening his fist in the man's shirt.

"I didn't mean to," the man muttered. "Here." He thrust the drill into Teddy's chest, forcing him to release his shirt to take the box, then took off running again. Teddy took a step after him.

"Wait," Flora said. "It's not worth it. He gave the drill back, at least. Thank you for helping, but I'd really rather this not devolve into violence."

"You should report him," Teddy grumbled, handing the drill over to her. She took the box and was relieved when he followed her back toward the store.

"I don't know his name. I'll let Grady know, though, and if he comes back, we'll do something about it."

"Oh, he'll come back all right," Teddy said, striding ahead to hold the hardware store door open for her. "He's Zeke Jefferson, a known troublemaker. I've had to deal with him stealing scrap, and I know other people who have had things stolen as well."

Flora grimaced. "Well, I'll let Officer Hendricks know, I guess. Let's get you checked out first."

She set the drill on the front counter before finishing the job of ringing him up at the register, calling out a final thanks as he went out the back door. The whole fiasco had put a damper on her day, but she cheered up a little when she saw Grady coming down the sidewalk just as Teddy left with his paint pails.

"Good morning," she said when he came in. "Did you walk to work?"

He gave her a quick hug in greeting then pulled back, sighed. "Yep. I let Wade borrow my truck to run some errands. He's supposed to be meeting me here with it. How's your day been?"

She told him about the attempted theft. "I suppose I should swing by the police station on my way home to report it. Do you know this Zeke guy?"

"He's a local," Grady said. "I think he used to work with Wade. We really should get some cameras put up, in case this happens again."

"Yeah, I'm just glad I saw him walking out. We're lucky he didn't use the back door. I wish Ellison was here – I don't like that I had to leave the store empty while Teddy and I went after him."

"When is he supposed to be in?"

"He's coming in this afternoon. Actually, he should be here any minute. What about –"

The electronic bell connected to the back door rang. She peeked down the aisle that led to the rear entrance and spotted a man with close-cropped hair the same color as Grady's but a little thinner striding down the aisle. He was muscular, and was wearing khaki pants and a polo shirt he looked uncomfortable in. Grady leaned against the counter next to Flora, crossing his arms.

"Is my truck in one piece?" he asked the man. She realized this must be his brother – the very person she was about to ask about — and felt a sudden thrill of nerves at the thought of finally meeting him.

"I don't think that thing's been in one piece since before dad died," the man said. "But it's in as good of shape as it was when you gave me the keys this morning." He paused and glanced around. "This place looks good. I like what you've done to it." His eyes landed on Flora, and he raised one of his eyebrows, apparently waiting for an introduction.

"Flora, this is my brother, Wade. Wade, my girlfriend and business partner, Flora."

"Nice to meet ya," Wade said, stepping closer so he could shake her hand. "Sounds like you've been helping my little brother out a lot. I appreciate it. How does a pretty girl like you come to own a hardware store?"

"I guess I was just in the right place at the right time," Flora said. "I wasn't exactly planning on it, but it's been fun. It's nice to meet you, I've heard a lot about you."

He chuckled. "All bad, I'm sure. I'm a changed man, though. Like I told Grady, the charges that put me in the prison might have been bogus, but I still turned over a new leaf while I was there. I'm going to be nothing but respectable from here on out." His gaze returned to Grady. "Sorry if I'm late. I ran into an old buddy on my way here. Got into a talk with him about maybe starting up the old business again. You remember Zeke, right?"

Grady tensed, and Flora felt her eyebrows go up. Zeke had to be Zeke Jefferson, the same man who had attempted to steal a drill just an hour ago. It wasn't too far-fetched that Wade might have spotted him while he was driving through town and pulled over to chat, but it didn't seem promising to her that an ex-convict was talking about business plans with a shoplifter.

"He's trouble," Grady said. "You're going to want to stay away from him."

"Zeke's harmless," Wade said, shaking his head. "But whatever you say. Here are your keys back. I'm going to take a walk around town and see who's hiring. I parked your truck around the back."

He dropped the keys into Grady's hand, nodded to

Flora, then left through the front door. Flora watched him go down the sidewalk.

"You didn't offer him a job here?" she asked, curious.

Grady shook his head. "Thought about it, but despite everything he's been saying about being a changed man, I'm not sure how much I trust him. I don't want to put the hardware store at risk. He'll figure something out, he still knows a lot of people around town and someone will be willing to take a chance on him. Maybe in the future, if he keeps his nose clean for a while, we can talk about offering him a position here."

Flora nodded, a little relieved that she wasn't going to have to get used to working with Grady's brother on top of training Ellison. Which reminded her…

"Where *is* Ellison? He's late. He was supposed to be here by noon." She checked the clock. It was ten after. He had only been working with them for a couple of weeks, but so far he had been on time every day.

"He must've got held up somewhere," Grady said. "You can head out if you want. I'll be fine here on my own. Thanks for opening today, by the way."

"I was happy to," she said. "I don't mind staying

for a while longer. Violet and I talked about grabbing lunch when she gets off at three. But I guess we don't need all three of us working until then. Maybe I'll get some shopping done – once Ellison finally shows up, that is." She sighed. "I've been on the register all morning. If you're okay to watch the front, I'll go empty the trash and maybe clean the windows or something."

"Are you sure you don't want me to do that?"

"I'm happy to do it myself. Like I said, I've been working the register all morning. I need to stretch my legs and do something more interesting than stand here and stare at the clouds outside."

She stopped by the supply closet and grabbed some empty garbage bags, then went around the store, emptying the bins. With a grunt of effort, she hefted all three of the full bags and carried them out back. After depositing them in the dumpster, she paused, looking around the parking lot in hopes of seeing Ellison's little blue sedan. She couldn't spot it anywhere, though she did see Grady's truck parked crookedly across two spots. She was about to turn around and go back inside when something else caught her eye.

There was a pickup truck parked not far from the rear entrance of the store, still running. It was parked facing away from her, and the tailgate was open. In the bed of the truck she could see pails of paint, just like the ones Teddy had bought earlier. She was certain the paint was Teddy's, but why was he still here? He should have left almost an hour ago.

Wondering if he needed to return the paint for some reason, or if he had come back to pick up something else, she walked around the side of the truck, then froze in place. The driver's side door was open, but the first thing that caught her eye was a hammer lying on the asphalt beside the front wheel. There was something dark around the head, something that looked a lot like blood. Slowly, she raised her eyes to look inside the truck. There, in the driver's seat, was Teddy Martin, slumped over the steering wheel, a bloody wound on his temple, and his bloodshot eyes open and staring at nothing.

CHAPTER FOUR

Flora stared at the scene until the sound of laughter from the street jolted her out of her shock. Slowly, she moved forward and placed her fingers on Teddy's neck. His skin was already cooling despite the warmth of the day, and she could tell that it was too late. He was gone.

Teddy Martin, the customer she had helped not even an hour ago, had been attacked and murdered in the hardware store's parking lot.

She took a few, shaky steps backward, then turned and ran toward the hardware store. She slammed through the door, ignoring the electronic ring of the bell, and hurried to the front counter. She had left her cell phone by the computer and grabbed it, not realizing Grady was talking to her until he said her name sharply.

"Flora! What's going on?"

She met the concerned look in his blue eyes and stumbled over her words. "In the parking lot... he's dead. Teddy. He's in his truck, I think someone hit him with a hammer–"

"Hey, slow down," he said, coming around the counter to put his hands on her shoulders. "Something happened in the parking lot? I'll go see. Are you going to be all right in here?"

She nodded. "I have to call the police. Don't... don't touch anything, all right?"

He nodded, gave her another concerned look, then hurried for the back door. While he went to go check on Teddy, she dialed the emergency number and took a deep breath before explaining what she had found to the dispatcher.

Grady came back in while they were still on the phone with her. He looked shaken, but he waited until the dispatcher confirmed that a unit was on the way before speaking.

"I didn't doubt you, but I had to see for myself," he said. "I can't believe it. How did no one notice? How long do you think he was out there?"

"It would've been almost an hour," she said. "Unless he came back for something."

"Geez. Teddy's been a regular here for a long time. It's hard to believe that's really him out there."

"Who would have done this?" she asked, making no pretense about how shaken she was. "I just... I don't understand. He was *right here*. He helped me with the attempted theft. He shouldn't be dead now."

He stepped forward and pulled her into a tight hug. "The police will figure it out. Maybe someone saw something. The parking lot isn't exactly private. There's a good chance they'll find a witness."

She took a deep breath and nodded. "Right. I guess all we can do is wait. Should we go out there and make sure no one else approaches the truck? We can lock up in here first." She didn't think they would be open for the rest of the day anyway. Not after this.

He nodded and together they shut down the computer and locked the front door. They went out the back door together and waited in the parking lot for the police to arrive. A squad car with two officers in it got there first, but an ambulance was right on its tail, and the paramedics rushed over to the truck to examine Teddy.

Flora didn't recognize the younger officer who got out of the squad car, but she recognized the other man who got out. Officer Hendricks. She counted him as a friendly acquaintance, though they rarely interacted outside of his job.

He nodded to her in greeting, but his attention was focused on Grady. "Mr. Barnes, I want to talk to you about something, but I'm going to take a look at our victim first."

They stood back and waited, watching as the paramedics called the time of death and let Officer Hendricks and the younger officer examine Teddy's body and the truck. They snapped some pictures, and then finally Officer Hendricks approached them again.

"I've got a feeling you might know what I'm about to ask you," he told Grady. "I heard your brother got out of prison. Has he been staying with you?"

"I'm the only family he's got," Grady said. "So yeah, he has."

"Do you know where he was today?"

Grady hesitated. "I lent him my truck so he could pick up some necessities, and he dropped it off here. He left on foot to see if anywhere local is hiring."

"And was this recent?"

"Yeah. He arrived sometime between when Teddy left the store and when Flora found him."

"I don't know if you're aware of this, Mr. Barnes, but Teddy Martin was the one who made the report that ended up getting your brother sent to prison. Normally, I wouldn't tell you this, but I know for a fact Wade already knows that tidbit. Some threats he made against Teddy in court affected his sentencing. So I'm not telling you anything new. Do you see what I'm getting at?"

"You think he did it. You think Wade killed Teddy."

"All I'm saying is, he's a suspect. He's got a grudge against the man, and the circumstantial evidence looks pretty bad. I'm going to leave Ralph here while I take a drive around town and look for him. If I leave you my card, will you give me a call when you see him? Right now, I just want to talk to him. If he cooperates with us, it's going to go a lot better for him."

Grady heaved a sigh. He sounded tired, and looked resigned as he spoke. "Yeah. I'll give you a call when I see him."

"You're a good man, Grady Barnes. I've come to see that over this past year. Don't let your brother drag you down with him."

With that, he left them alone, going over to talk to

the younger officer. Flora bit her lip, looking at Grady out of the corner of her eye.

Had his brother shown his true colors already? Had he really killed a man so soon after getting out of prison?

CHAPTER FIVE

Officer Hendricks notified them that the parking lot would need to be closed while the forensics team did their investigation, and after a brief chat, she and Grady decided to close the hardware store down for the next couple of days. It would be too much hassle to try to keep people from using the back lot, and it felt like the respectful thing to do anyway. A man had been murdered. The least they could do was to keep from making a spectacle of his death.

She didn't have it in her to meet Violet for lunch, so she told her friend she would explain everything later and went straight home instead. Focusing on the house always helped her feel better, so she installed the new hardware she had bought in the upstairs bathroom.

Her eyes lingered on the stained grout between the tiles on the floor. She had tried every trick in the book but still couldn't get it clean. Not for the first time, she wondered if she should replace the floor, but she had watched more than one video on replacing tile and it looked like a messy, hard job. But at the same time, was there any reason not to do it? She couldn't let herself get too distracted by the hardware store. Her main focus had to be the house, if she ever wanted to make a career of this. And she did – while she greatly enjoyed working at the hardware store and had no plans to sell her portion of the business, what she really loved was her work on the house.

"The tiles themselves would probably be pretty cheap," she muttered, frowning at the floor. "I mean, I get discounts on almost everything if I buy through the hardware store. And it would look really nice with new tile in here…"

She sighed and made a mental note to add replacing the tiles to her list. And if she was going to do the upstairs bathroom, she might as well do the downstairs one too.

Despite her initial reluctance to commit to the project, as she returned downstairs, she felt a familiar glimmer of excitement. The project might be a pain to work on, but she knew she wouldn't regret doing it.

If, when the time came, she couldn't get the amount she wanted from the sale of the house, she wanted to be able to say that she had done the best she possibly could.

She spent the rest of the evening looking at tile options online and checking Warbler's social media page to see if anyone was saying anything about Teddy Martin's death. There were a few posts asking why the hardware store parking lot was cordoned off, but that was it. She didn't know whether to be disappointed or glad that no one had any other information. She supposed it was a good thing – she knew Grady wouldn't want his family's business posted all over the internet, and besides, if she wanted real information, she could just go to the source.

She waited until after dinner to call Grady. As the phone rang, she began to wonder if it was going to go to voicemail, but he picked up on what must have been the last ring.

"Hey," he said. "No update yet. I have a feeling that's what you're calling for. Wade hasn't been home, and I haven't heard from the police."

"I see. I hope everything gets straightened out soon. This waiting around can't be fun."

"I just hope he hasn't left town. I guess I should be glad that he gave the truck back first, if he did."

"Do you think…" She hesitated.

"Do I think he did it? I don't know what to say. I know he's got a questionable past, but I never thought of him as a dangerous man. He was always all bark and no bite when we were kids, you know? But I've got to remember, he isn't the same man I knew before. Spending years behind bars would change anyone. He said it changed him for the better, but I don't know how true that is."

"Sorry, Grady. Just… call me if you want to talk, all right? You're welcome to come over too."

"Thanks, but I'd better stay here in case he comes home."

They said their goodbyes and she ended the call. Flora's mood was somber as she went to bed that night. She felt terrible for Teddy, and for Grady too. How terrible must it be to not know whether a loved one was guilty of a crime as dark as murder?

She woke up the next morning to the feel of her cat's sharp claws kneading her stomach. She moved Amaretto off of her with a groan. "I've got to cut your nails, sweetie. That hurts."

Undeterred, the cat rolled onto her back, making a cute chirping sound that just about melted Flora's heart.

"Okay, that's adorable. I forgive you. What do

you say we go get some breakfast? Then we can take a walk out back and see how hard it will be to cut a path through all of that brush toward the pond."

Since she wasn't going into town today, she turned the coffee maker on and served Amaretto her breakfast while she waited for her drink to finish being made. Just as the coffee machine was gurgling its last few drops, her phone started ringing. She could hear the sound faintly from down the hall, and realized she had left it upstairs. Hoping it might be Grady with an update, she leapt to her feet and raced toward the stairs. She made it to her room just as the call went to voicemail.

Picking it up, she saw the caller had indeed been Grady and quickly redialed his number.

"Hey," she said as soon as she heard him pick up. "Sorry, I was making coffee. I didn't bring my phone downstairs with me. Is everything all right?"

"Wade finally came home late last night. I told him what happened and he agreed to go down to the police station with me this morning."

"And? Did they arrest him?"

He heaved a sigh. "They're keeping him in custody for the time being. I don't know why or what was said, but I told him I'd help him find a lawyer. I just… I don't know what to think, Flora. He told me he didn't do it. But if he's really innocent, why would the police be holding him?"

"I'm sorry, Grady. I don't know what to say. What does your gut tell you? Do you think he did it?"

"Honestly, after talking to him last night... I don't think he had anything to do with it. I don't know if I'm being stupid, trusting him, especially since he swore he was innocent of the drug charges that got him into prison as well, but I know my brother. I think he was telling the truth when I talked to him last night."

"Then I'll help you," she said. "Even if there isn't enough evidence for the police to keep him in custody, with the way this town is, he's never going to find a job or be able to rebuild his life here if people think he killed someone. We need to figure out who killed Teddy Martin."

CHAPTER SIX

Grady told her he was going to start looking into lawyers, though he wasn't sure if he would be able to contact any of them since it was a Sunday. Flora, for her part, decided to do some information gathering… which sounded a lot better than what she was really going to do; gossip with her neighbor, Beth.

Beth York had lived in Warbler all her life, and knew everything there was to know about the town, or that was how it seemed. She was always more than happy to share the latest gossip, and Flora thought talking to her would be a good place to start.

She had time to finish a few tasks on her chore list first, though. After drinking her coffee and getting ready for the day, she took Amaretto's harness and leash down from the coat tree by the front door and put the harness on her cat. Training Amaretto to be comfortable in the harness had been a long process, but the cat loved going outdoors, and now walking her was almost as easy as walking a dog — assuming she and Amaretto agreed on which direction they wanted to go. If Flora tried to go somewhere the cat wasn't interested in, Amaretto would flop over onto her side and refuse to move.

"Are you ready to help me with some work today?" Flora asked the cat as she slipped her shoes on and unlocked the door. "We're going out back to the woods. I think you'll enjoy it."

She opened the door and let Amaretto strut outside first. The cat paused on the porch and looked around, her ears twitching as she took in the morning. After letting the cat adjust for a few seconds, Flora made kissing sounds and led her slowly around to the back of the house, where the shed was. Here, she paused to grab the orange marker flags she wanted to use to mark out what would become a path to the pond.

Walking with the cat was always slow going, and she paused more than a few times to let Amaretto sniff at a spot on the ground or stare up at a bird as it flew by, but before too long they reached the tree line, and she set two markers where she wanted the entrance of the path to be. She thought it was about where the old path had been — she knew the pond used to be a popular swimming hole for the local kids and teens — but it was long since overgrown.

She took her time walking through the woods, pausing every few steps to plant more flags to mark out the path or let Amaretto explore. It was mid-morning by the time she finished, setting the last two flags a few feet away from the muddy bank of the pond. She stared at the murky water for a few seconds, trying to envision how it would look when it was cleaned out. She could bring some sand in to make the banks nicer, and maybe even install a little gazebo. Hiring someone else to build one would be out of the question, but between her discount at the hardware store, all of the free instructional videos she could find online, and help from her friends in exchange for free food and plenty of summer nights spent hanging out in said gazebo, she thought she might be able to build one on her own.

Satisfied that she had gotten at least a little bit of work done – now that she had the path marked out, she could either pay someone to clear it or borrow a brush cutter herself – she scooped up Amaretto, who was rolling in a patch of something that smelled like catnip, and walked back to her house.

After taking Amaretto's harness off and giving the cat a few treats, she grabbed her phone and keys and let herself back out of the house, locking the door behind her. Then, she headed down the dirt road toward her closest neighbor's house. It was a good quarter of a mile walk. The sheer solitude of the area had been astonishing to her when she first moved here, having lived in Chicago for all of her life before that. She had gotten used to it by now, and had come to value and appreciate the privacy and quiet of her country home.

When she finally reached the Yorks' property, she strode across the grass to the front porch. Climbing the steps, she knocked on the front door and waited. It wasn't long before Beth opened the front door. Her wrinkled face creased into a bright smile when she saw Flora.

"What a lovely surprise. Why don't you come in, dear?"

"Thanks, Beth," Flora said. She made to take her shoes off, but the older woman paused her with a hand on her arm.

"Actually, before you get too comfortable, do you think you could give me a lift to the feed store? I forgot to add Sammy's food to the list when I went shopping yesterday, and I need to pick up another bag. I can pay for the gas, of course."

Sammy was their Basset hound, a droopy, calm dog that Beth walked down the road and back again multiple times each day. Beth and her husband, Tim, were both too old to drive, so they didn't have a car. There was a small bus that took Beth into town to shop every Saturday, and if she needed to go to an appointment or pick up groceries any other time, she called one of her friends for a ride. Flora didn't think she would like being stuck out here without a car, but it seemed to work for the older couple.

"Oh, of course. And no need to pay me for anything. I walked over here; do you want me to run back and get my truck?"

"I hate to put you out, but that would probably be faster than waiting for me to walk over to your house. I'll get ready to go while you get it. You're such a peach, Flora."

It took her a few minutes to jog back to her house and retrieve her purse from inside. By the time she pulled into Beth's driveway, the older woman standing on the porch, waiting for her. Flora unlocked the passenger door and waited while Beth got in.

"Just the feed store, or do you need anything else?"

"Just the dog food, I think," Beth said. "Before I forget, what did you want to talk to me about? You must have had something on your mind when you came over."

Beth was kind enough not to mention that Flora rarely initiated any of their visits. She felt a pang of guilt for the reminder, and resolved to make more of an effort to visit the other woman just for a friendly chat every now and then.

"Well, I don't know if you heard what happened at the hardware store yesterday," she said as she guided the truck toward the main road. "Teddy Martin was murdered in the parking lot."

"One of the women in my book club called to tell me about that," Beth said, a sharp glint in her eyes as she latched onto the subject. "I wasn't sure how accurate her information was. That's just horrible, Flora. I hope you and that nice Barnes boy weren't too affected. You didn't see the body, did you?"

"I'm the one who found him," Flora said grimly. "I just wish I knew who did it. Grady's brother just got out of prison, you see, and the police think it's him."

Beth looked even more interested than before. "Oh dear, he's out already? It was big news around town when he got that conviction years ago. You be careful around him. He is the black sheep of that family. Grady might be a nice boy, but his brother sure isn't. The police know what they're doing, especially when it comes to a man like him."

That wasn't what Flora was hoping to hear. "You really think he could have done it? Because Grady talked to him about it, and he seems to believe his brother is innocent."

Beth reached over and patted her hand gently. "Of course he does, dear. It's his brother we're talking about. Family sticks together, especially out here. Try not to follow your heart on this one, Flora. A man was murdered, and it happened when a convicted felon returned to town. I know you want to support your friend, but sometimes we have to listen to the facts rather than our emotions."

Flora hit the blinker to turn toward town, mulling over Beth's response. She wanted to believe Grady about his brother's innocence, she really did, but even *he* had been hesitant to say whether or not he believed Wade. Despite having been here for a year, Flora was still a newcomer. She didn't know much about Wade's history in town, or what his past was like besides the fact that he had been convicted of a drug-related charge serious enough to put him in prison for years. As much as she hated to admit it, Beth might have a point.

"I mostly just don't want it to be true for Grady's sake," she admitted as the truck sped toward Warbler. "He seemed nice enough when I met him, I guess, but I have to admit, it does look pretty bad for him."

"The most important thing is that you keep yourself safe," Beth said. "Let Grady deal with his brother. You should stay out of this, Flora."

CHAPTER SEVEN

She wasn't sure whether to count her attempt at information gathering as a failure or not. She hadn't gotten the information she wanted, but that didn't mean Beth hadn't given good advice. When they reached the main intersection in town, she turned right, heading toward the feed store. The ride was mostly quiet – thankfully, Beth seemed to sense that she needed time to think.

When they arrived at the store, they got out and went inside together. Beth grabbed a cart and headed toward the dog food section, but Flora paused at the front counter to say hi to Sydney, Violet's boyfriend, and one of Flora's closest friends in town.

She exchanged a brief greeting with him before

realizing Beth was here to buy *dog food* – which meant there was probably going to be a heavy bag and some lifting involved. She hurried off to help Beth lift the bag into the cart, then pushed it back to the counter and chatted with Sydney while Beth paid.

"I put in an order for some of that food your cat likes so much," Sydney told her as he handed Beth her change. "I know how picky she is. It should be in on Friday."

"Thanks, Sydney," Flora said. Her musings on building a gazebo felt very far away, but she knew she couldn't put her work on the house on hold while she and Grady dealt with the mess Wade was in. "I've got some plans for the summer I want to talk to everyone about, so let me know what days you're free this week and I'll see about getting everyone together."

"I will," he promised. "Have a good day, both of you."

She pushed the cart outside for Beth and walked around to the back of her truck. Opening the tailgate, she heaved the heavy bag of kibble into the bed. When she reached for the cart to bring it back into the store, Beth shooed her away.

"I appreciate your help, dear, but I'm not an invalid yet. Let me at least take this back inside. You've already done more than enough."

Flora leaned against the side of her truck, watching as Beth pushed the cart back through the parking lot and toward the store. She felt at loose ends. Today was technically supposed to be a day off, but she felt too unsettled by the murder to relax. She needed something to focus on.

The sound of another car pulling into the parking lot got her attention, and she turned to see a blue sedan approaching her. It was Ellison. She felt a jolt of relief that he was okay, along with guilt when she remembered that she hadn't even *thought* about him since the murder. She wondered if he had shown up, late for his shift, only to find the store closed and the parking lot cordoned off with crime scene tape.

He parked his car in the spot next to her truck and got out, leaning with his elbows on the roof of the car as he looked over it to talk to her.

"Sorry to ambush you like this, Ms. Abner, but I saw you while I was driving past. Mr. Barnes called me this morning and told me the hardware store was going to be closed for the next couple of days, but he ended the call before I could get any details. I tried texting him, but didn't get a response. What's going on?"

"Yeah, getting him to respond to text messages is like pulling teeth," Flora said. "Your best bet is to call

him, or just text or call me if you need something."
She hesitated. She didn't want to give out personal
information about Grady's brother or any specific
details about what had happened, in case the police
wanted to keep it quiet. "There was a death in the
parking lot, and the police are still investigating. I'm
sorry you had to find out this way. I think we're planning on reopening Wednesday, but I'm not sure." She
paused. "You didn't go to the store yesterday afternoon at all?"

"Nah, I was out of town," he said. "I don't usually
stop by when I'm not working, anyway. I live in an
apartment, so there isn't exactly much maintenance I
can do myself, and I think my landlord would kick me
out if I tried to paint the walls or something."

She frowned. "You were out of town? I thought
you were scheduled to work yesterday."

He gave her a puzzled look. "No. I had the day
off. I think I have a picture of the schedule on my
phone…"

She shook her head. "Don't worry about it. I must
have been wrong about the schedule. It's probably a
good thing you weren't there, anyway. It was a mess."

"Do you know who died? Was it, like, an accident
or something?"

"Teddy Martin," she said. "I don't know if you know him. He's a regular, and owns a scrap metal recycling business. He was murdered. Someone attacked him with a hammer."

To her surprise, Ellison's expression darkened. "Oh, I know him all right, but not from the store. My parents got into a big dispute with him last year – he stole the chassis of some fancy classic car my dad owned right off their lawn. He said he thought it was scrap that they wanted him to take away, but it was worth a lot of money. They never got it back." He winced. "Not that I'm saying I'm glad about what happened to him or anything."

The doors to the feed store slid open and Beth came out, heading toward the truck. Flora shifted, pushing away from the truck and getting her keys ready.

"Well, one of us will be in contact with you. I'm hoping it won't be too long, just another day or two."

He nodded and got back into his car just as Beth arrived. She let the other woman into the truck silently, thoughts buzzing in her head.

Teddy had seemed like a perfectly normal man. He had helped her *prevent* a theft, for goodness sakes. It was hard to imagine him stealing from Ellison's family. But in a strange way, her employee's words had given her hope. If Teddy Martin had more enemies around town than just Wade, maybe Grady's brother wasn't the killer after all.

CHAPTER EIGHT

After dropping Beth back off at her house, Flora returned home, still feeling at odds with herself. She didn't want to sit on the couch and do nothing, but she also wasn't feeling inspired about working on the house anymore. She wanted to talk to Grady, but she didn't want to interrupt him while he was busy hunting for a good lawyer for Wade.

In the end, she busied herself with looking up gazebo designs online and watching videos about how to build one herself. She made a list of things she would need to do and the permits she would need to get for the construction, and then spent the rest of the day alternating between reading and watching the news.

She woke up bright and early Monday morning

with her phone ringing all too cheerfully from her nightstand. She reached for it blindly and squinted to hit the right button to answer it, spotting Grady's name on the caller ID.

"Hello?" she said groggily.

"Good morning," he said. "Did I wake you up?"

She glanced at the clock on her nightstand. It was just past nine in the morning. Grady, she knew, woke up ridiculously early from years of having the opening shift at the hardware store before the previous owner passed away.

Flora liked to sleep in. She felt a peculiar sense of shame about it, especially since all of her closest friends were early risers.

"Nope," she lied, trying to sound chipper. "I've been up for hours."

He chuckled. "I'll pretend to believe that. Do you have any plans today?"

"I was thinking about trying to rent some equipment, but it's nothing urgent. What's up? How is Wade doing? Did you find a lawyer for him?"

She sat up in bed, idly petting Amaretto, feeling more awake now as she remembered all of the things she had to worry about.

"I managed to contact a lawyer who got back to me earlier this morning, and is on his way to meet with Wade. It's going to be expensive, so right now he's just going to advise Wade. He might have to use a public defender if it goes to court. I was wondering if you want to meet up and talk about all this and maybe go visit an old friend of Wade's with me. I'd like to get some more information on the history between him and Teddy."

"Sure," she said. "Though… no offense to your brother, but I know he's got a bit of the past. Is this friend… safe?"

He hesitated. "I don't think he's dangerous, but you're not going to like it. It's Zeke Jefferson."

"*Really*?" she said. "I literally ran him down for shoplifting two days ago. I don't think he's going to want to talk to me."

"He knows I own the hardware store too. I don't think he's going to want to talk to either of us, but he was Wade's best friend before my brother went to prison. He was a part of all the stuff that happened with Teddy and the charges that got Wade put behind bars. If anyone knows more about it than I do, it's him. I was hoping we could get out there early and catch him before he leaves his house. Wade says he still lives in the same place, and gave me his address."

"I'll go with you," she said. "Do you want to meet in town, or pick me up?"

"I'll pick you up. I'll be there in about half an hour. Will that give you enough time to get ready?"

She gave a playful scoff. "Ready? I told you, I've already been up for hours."

Despite her reservations, she grinned as she ended the call and jumped out of bed to hurry through her morning routine. By the time Grady pulled into her driveway, she had two warm thermoses of coffee in her hands and was feeling much more alert. She hurried to get into the truck before Grady could get out to open the passenger side door for her, and handed him one of the thermoses.

"Let's get going," she said. As he pulled out of the driveway, she added, "Oh, I forgot to tell you, I tried to do some snooping yesterday, and I talked to Beth."

"What did she have to say?"

Flora sighed. "Nothing helpful, I'm afraid. She is pretty convinced Wade did it."

Grady snorted. "I'm not surprised. Honestly, while I want to think he's innocent, that's not the same as being *sure* he is. I'm not going to be surprised if it turns out he did it after all. Disappointed, but not surprised."

"Well, hopefully Zeke will be able to shed some light on all of this," she said as he guided the truck towards town. "That is, if he'll talk to us."

Zeke Jefferson lived in a rundown house on the outskirts of town. There was old, rusty scrap metal all over the yard, and Flora watched her step as they traversed the uncut grass to the front porch. Grady went first, pounding on the screen door before stepping back and crossing his arms. She fidgeted – part of her wished she hadn't agreed to come along, but at the same time, she knew she couldn't leave Grady to question a potentially dangerous man on his own.

The door opened and Zeke glared out at them. His eyes flicked between her face and Grady's. "What?" he snapped. "I didn't take anything else. If you're here to look for some items you misplaced, you can take a hike."

"We aren't here for that," Grady said. "It's about Wade. Can we come in?"

The other man frowned. "I know you're his brother and all, Grady, but I don't want either of you in my house. For all I know, you're going to go sniffing around looking for something to strengthen your case with the police. You should remember that I didn't *actually* take anything. You got that drill back. You don't have a case against me."

"I didn't go to the police about it," Flora volunteered. It was true – the attempted shoplifting had been the last thing on her mind after finding Teddy's body. She hadn't even thought to mention it to Officer Hendricks when he responded to the call. She wasn't happy he had tried to steal from the hardware store, but murder was in a different category entirely. "We really do just want to talk to you about Wade. He's in trouble. Isn't he your friend?"

Zeke hesitated, then pushed the screen door open, stepping out onto the deck and crossing his arms, in a mirror of Grady's posture.

"Fine, if you want to talk, then talk."

"You don't want to sit down?" Grady asked. "This might take a while."

"You can either talk or you can get off my property."

Grady sighed. "Well, I was hoping you could tell us more about what happened with Teddy and Wade back when he got arrested for drug possession."

Zeke snorted. "You're a bit too late for that, aren't you? Where were you when your brother was looking at prison time for a crime he didn't commit?"

"I was at home, thinking about all the other times my brother got in trouble with the law," Grady retorted. "I'm here now, isn't that what matters?"

"Well, what did he get pinched for this time?"

Flora exchanged a glance with Grady. It hadn't

occurred to her Zeke might not know about what happened.

"Homicide," Grady said grimly. "The murder of Teddy Martin. He made some threats to him in court that went on record, and he was caught near the scene of the crime. It looks bad for him, but he insists he didn't do it and I'm trying to figure out the truth. I know Teddy was involved in his previous arrest. What can you tell me about that?"

Zeke frowned. "Involved is one way to put it. Teddy planted those drugs in Wade's truck. You remember the business we were trying to start up at the time? Hauling and recycling scrap metal for people. Teddy was our main competitor, and he didn't like that we were getting so much business. With Wade behind bars, I couldn't keep up with it on my own, and our business crashed while his took off. I wouldn't blame Wade for wanting a little revenge. I'm not trying to say I think he killed the man, and I wouldn't repeat this if the cops asked me, but far as I'm concerned, Teddy got what was coming to him."

"I know I'm not exactly local, but from what I saw of Teddy, he seemed… Well, pretty normal. Do you really think he framed Wade for a crime and masterminded some plot to drive the two of you out of business?" Flora asked.

Zeke scoffed. "Teddy puts on a good face to the public, but he is no angel. Most of the reviews for his business are good if you look it up online, but that's because he keeps a close eye on the page and removes all the ones that aren't. If you keep your ear to the ground, you'll hear complaints about him taking scrap that doesn't belong to him, him offering lowball prices to people who don't know what they have, all sorts of scummy stuff. And besides, he planted those drugs on Wade. I believe that completely. Your brother was really trying to turn over a new leaf when we started that business. And drugs don't just grow on trees, not even around here. Do you think a perfectly normal, clean family man would know how to source enough drugs to put someone behind bars for years?" He shook his head. "Look, I don't want anything to do with this. I won't mess with your store again. I was desperate, you understand? Mine kicked the bucket over the weekend, and I needed a new one for work. I talked to you like you wanted. Now, can we just drop the whole thing?"

Grady glanced at Flora, a question in his eyes. She hesitated, then shrugged. A part of her felt like they should report the attempted crime to the police, but when it came down to it – she was tired. It was obvious that Zeke really was down on his luck, and nothing had been damaged or lost. Besides, she got the feeling that him talking to them like this was a favor he expected to be repaid by them not pressing charges.

"Just don't let it happen again," Grady said. "Thanks for the chat. Before we go, if Wade didn't do it – do you have any idea who would have?"

Zeke shrugged, leaning back against the side of his house. "Who knows? It's not your job to figure it out. I suggest minding your own business. No one likes a snoop. Doubt your brother would want you getting hurt trying to help him."

With that, he turned around and went back into his house, the screen door slamming shut behind him.

CHAPTER NINE

"Grady," Flora said as they got back into the truck. "He didn't say your brother *didn't* do it. If what he's saying is true, Wade had a good reason to have a grudge against Teddy."

Grady started the truck and reversed out of Zeke's driveway with a little too much force.

"I know," he grunted.

"We can keep asking around, but Wade was right there – he came in through the back of the store from the parking lot Teddy was killed in."

"I know," he said with a sigh. "I don't know what to tell you, Flora. I know what it looks like. I don't know what to think. Not anymore. You didn't see him the night he came home and I told him about Teddy's death. I really did believe him then. But I just don't know what to think anymore. But if he gets put behind bars again, I want to know for sure it's because of something he did."

"Do you think Zeke was right, and he was framed for the drug charges?"

He frowned. "A part of me doesn't want to think about it," he admitted quietly. "Back then, he tried to get me to believe that he was innocent. A lot like this time, in fact. And I didn't. He had been in trouble before, and it fit with what I knew about him. But after all these years, he's still adamant that he didn't do it, and after hearing Zeke out… I just don't know what to think. I feel like I owe it to him to try to figure out the truth though, no matter what it is. You don't have to keep helping me."

"No, I want to," she said. "I said I would. I just don't know what to do next."

"I think I've got to go talk to Wade again," Grady said. "Maybe he'll change his tune, or maybe he'll have some new information we can use." He hesitated. "I don't know if they'll let us both in to see him."

"It's all right," she said. "I'm not particularly eager to see the inside of a jail, anyway."

He nodded, and they sat mostly in silence as he drove her back home.

She stood in her driveway, waving as he drove away, her heart heavy. She understood this was hard for him, and tried to put herself in his shoes. Neither of her siblings were the sort to do anything that might get them in trouble with the law, but if one of them was being held by the police for a crime they said they didn't commit, she would be a complete mess. And she would be angry at how unfair it all was. Grady didn't seem angry. He just seemed sad. It was hard to help him when she didn't know how. She needed to talk to someone else, get another viewpoint on it.

She texted Violet as she went inside, asking if her friend wanted to meet up later this afternoon. While she waited for a reply, she got online and found a company in the next town over that rented equipment, including the brush cutter that she needed to clear the path through the forest. She could rent it for the week for only a couple hundred dollars. Depending on how easy it was to get through all of that brush, she might be able to make more than one path. Having a few walking paths through the forest would be nice, and once she got the worst of the brush removed, she should be able to maintain it with her lawnmower.

After a quick call during which she ran out to her truck to double check the dimensions of the bed to be sure the machine would fit in it, she grabbed her purse again and headed out, eager to have something to do besides sit around and worry about Wade and Grady.

She was halfway to the next town when Violet texted her back. She used the wireless function on her truck to read the text message out to her, then responded by dictating a new message, agreeing to meet Violet at the new cheesesteak restaurant just after three.

Flora's favorite sandwich shop had shut down after the owner was murdered, and a new place had opened up to take its spot. She had been there a couple of times, and while the cheesesteaks they served were good, they were greasy and left Flora feeling a little gross for the rest of the day.

Today felt like a day for some self-indulgence, though. She swung by the rental company and picked up the brush cutter, then headed back to Warbler, stopping to get gas while she waited for Violet to get out of work. She pulled up to the cheesesteak restaurant a few minutes past three and went inside to get a table. Violet arrived a few minutes later.

"Hey," her friend said cheerfully. "I saw that big beast of a machine in the back of your truck. Are you finally tackling the pond?"

"I'm planning on it," Flora said. "The guy at the

store gave me some instructions on how to operate this, but I'm still a little worried I might accidentally cut off my foot or something. It will be nice to have this done, though. I spent most of last year focusing on the interior of the house. I think having more amenities in the yard will really boost the interest I get when I post it for sale."

"I agree," Violet said as she picked up one of the paper menus. "Especially for people with kids. That property is the perfect place to raise a little family. I know I would've loved growing up on a few acres with a pond and paths through the woods, and a nice big yard like you have."

Flora could imagine it, and felt a pang at the thought that she would never get to raise her own children there. She tried to always keep in the forefront of her mind that her life at the house was only temporary, but somewhere along the way, she had fallen in love with the place. It was going to be hard to let it go.

"So, I only heard the basics. What's all this going on with the homicide and Grady's brother?"

Flora took a deep breath and started to fill her in. As she spoke, she felt some of the tension ease out of her shoulders.

Violet wasn't going to be able to help her and

Grady solve the crime. She might be able to listen to rumors for them, but she'd never been close to Wade or any of the other people involved. What she *could* do was listen, and that was all Flora needed right now. Someone to listen, someone to understand how hard all of this was. She suspected that Wade wasn't as innocent as he claimed, and she had been beginning to wonder if they were doing the right thing, digging for answers on a case that seemed so open and shut.

Violet reminded her that she wasn't doing this for Wade. She was doing it for Grady, who needed to know that if his brother ended up getting a life sentence, it was because he deserved it, and not just because he had been in the wrong place at the wrong time.

CHAPTER TEN

Her new resolve about helping Grady didn't do anything for the butterflies she had in her stomach when she woke up the next morning. Angry butterflies. More like wasps, really.

Grady was visiting his brother in the local jail this morning, and she didn't know if Wade would have anything new to say. He and Grady might just be going around in circles right now. If Wade still claimed to be innocent, with no new information, then they would be back at square one. She wanted to help Grady find evidence either way of his brother's innocence or guilt, but she didn't know what else to do.

It was nearly noon when her phone rang. She was outside, raking away some of the debris from the first few feet of the path she had cut with the brush cutter, and dropped the rake in her haste to answer the call, feeling a flash of relief at the sight of Grady's name on the screen.

"Hey," she said. "How did it go?"

"He hasn't changed his tune," Grady said. "He still says he's innocent. I know it looks bad, but my gut tells me he's telling the truth. He seems positive. Keeps talking about what he's going to do when he gets out." He gave a dry laugh. "Even said that he was going to see if he could buy Teddy's scrap business, now that Teddy won't be needing it anymore. I don't know how he knows, but he said Teddy's nephew owns the place, and he thinks he'll be able to convince him to sell."

"Geez, if anything, that just makes it sound like he has even more of a motive for murder," Flora said. "The police must be having a field day. First they have him on record threatening Teddy while he was in court, and now he's talking about wanting to buy the victim's business. You did say you found a lawyer for him, right?"

"Yeah, and they met once already. I'm sure he's not thrilled with the way Wade is handling this. I was thinking, maybe we should go talk to Teddy's nephew ourselves. I'll go on my own, if you've got things to do."

"No, I can come," Flora said, eyeing the brush and weeds she still had to cut through. Since she had to return the machine in a week, she did have a deadline to get this done, but helping Grady was more important.

"Do you want me to swing by and pick you up?"

"Sure," she said. "Are we still planning on reopening the hardware store tomorrow? One of us should call Ellison."

"Yeah, I can do that after I get off the phone with you," he said.

"No, you're driving. I'll do it. When will you be here?"

"In about forty minutes," he said. "If you need help with anything when we're done, I'm happy to spend the evening there."

"Thanks, I might take you up on that."

She said a quick goodbye, then navigated through her contacts list and clicked on Ellison's name. He answered, sounding distracted.

"Hey, Ellison. I just talked to Grady, and we are still going to be reopening tomorrow. I don't have the schedule in front of me, but I think you were scheduled to come in in the morning. Can you still do that?"

"Yeah, no problem, Ms. Abner," he said. "Oh, do they know who killed that guy yet?"

"No, they're still working on it," she told him.

"Have you heard anything about any leads or suspects?" he asked. He sounded like he was paying more attention now. The music she had heard playing in the background stopped.

"I know they have at least one suspect," she said, though she didn't want to bring up Wade's name just in case he was innocent after all.

"Cool, cool," he said. She thought he sounded a little nervous.

"Is everything all right? If you're worried about whoever killed Teddy coming back to the store, we can figure something out. In fact, we should probably make sure no one works there alone until we know who the culprit is."

"Nah, I'm sure it will be all right, Ms. Abner," he said. "Though if I see any suspicious people approaching me with a hammer, I'd like your permission to peace out."

She chuckled. "Permission granted. And that goes for any time you're working – if anyone seems dangerous or is even just giving off weird vibes, get somewhere safe and call one of us or the police. I don't want anyone getting hurt."

"Thanks, Ms. Abner. I'll see you tomorrow."

He said a quick goodbye and ended the call. Flora tucked her phone back into her pocket and stooped to grab her rake, then paused.

Had she told him about the hammer? She couldn't remember. She might have – she *must* have. She didn't think the police had released any information about the murder weapon.

She must have told him. Swallowing heavily against the worm of doubt that was creeping into her mind, she resumed clearing the path. She had forty minutes until Grady got here, and she wanted to make the most of it.

Teddy's business was to the south of town, a few miles past where the turnoff to the road she lived on was. Grady knew the way, and she rode contentedly in the passenger seat as he drove them there. A chain link fence surrounded the junkyard, and the gate was closed. There were piles of metal scattered all about, and a modular home that seemed to double as the office sat in one of the few clear areas. Grady parked in front of the gate and they got out.

"This place looks abandoned," she said. "Well,

there are a lot of cars here, but they all look like junk."

"That one has a license plate with a current tag on it," he said, nodding toward a blue SUV that was parked in front of the office building. It was beat up and rusty, but it did look like it was parked instead of dumped there.

Grady reached for the gate and pulled it open far enough that they could slip through, then shut it behind them. Flora froze as a large, black dog raced toward them from around a pile of metal, barking ferociously. Before the dog reached them, the door to the office building opened and a man stepped out.

"Shadow," he shouted. "Leave it. Come here."

The dog slowed and sniffed at them, then turned and trotted back toward the man.

"He won't hurt you, he just likes to bark," the man called out. "We're closed, though. You're going to have to call and leave a message if you want something."

"Are you Teddy Martin's nephew?" Grady called back. "We're here to talk, not for business."

The man hesitated, but after second, he waved them over. "Come on in, and don't mind Shadow. He'll sniff you all over, but he won't hurt you."

Sure enough, the dog took its time sniffing Flora's

shoes and pants before moving on to Grady while they stood in the man's office.

"I'm Hunter Martin," the man said, shaking their hands. "What is this about?"

"We are here to talk about your uncle," Grady said. "It's a legal matter. We are trying –"

"No," Hunter sighed immediately, taking a step back. "I'm not handling any of that. We have a lawyer, and I can put you in touch with her. I can't help you."

"You don't even know what we want," Flora said.

"I can guess. You might not have heard, but he has passed away. His estate is tied up right now, and any claims will have to go through official channels."

"We're trying to figure out who killed him," Flora said quickly, before he could keep making assumptions. Then she paused, remembering something Ellison had told her. "Has he been having legal issues?"

"You… aren't here about that?" Hunter looked relieved. "He's had a lot of complaints, it felt like I was getting calls every week about it. Ever since that Adams' lawsuit, it's been crazy. They must have a lot of friends in town, because people have been absolutely hounding us."

"Adams?" Grady asked, looking puzzled. Flora

realized that she hadn't told him about the issues Ellison's parents had with Teddy. "What was that about?"

Hunter hesitated, then shrugged. "I guess it's all public knowledge. They hired us to clear some scrap out of their yard – old, broken-down cages, wire from the garden, springs for mattresses they burned, that sort of thing. They left it all in a heap by an old car chassis, and weren't very clear about what we should take. Teddy swung by with the trailer and took the car too, found out it was worth the money, and sold it. By the time they contacted us to complain, it was gone. They sued us and lost. Ever since, they've been getting all of their friends to make complaints against us. It's been a real pain. Hopefully, they'll stop now that my uncle's gone. Why do you want to know, anyway?"

"We're trying to figure out what happened to your uncle," Grady said. "I'm Grady Barnes, and I'm part owner of the hardware –"

Immediately, Hunter backed away from him. "I know who you are. Your brother's the one the police took into custody. I don't want anything to do with you. Get out of here."

"We just want to talk," Flora said. "Please, we're trying to figure out –"

"No," Hunter said. By his side, Shadow growled.

"Leave, or I'm going to call the police and report you for trespassing."

That didn't give them much of an option. They left, having wasted a trip into town and once again, no better off than they were before.

CHAPTER ELEVEN

On their way back to Flora's house, she told Grady all about her impromptu meeting with Ellison at the feed store.

"Sorry, it completely slipped my mind with everything else going on. I think it's just a coincidence that his parents had issues with Teddy." She hesitated, biting her lip. "You don't think he had something to do with it, do you? I could have sworn he was scheduled to work that day, even though he said he had the day off."

Grady frowned, concentrating on the road. "I thought he was scheduled as well. Have you checked the schedule?"

"No, I didn't have it saved on my phone. I'll check it when we go back to the hardware store tomorrow. If he was lying, well, I'm not sure what it will mean."

Had Ellison shown up there for his shift, only to run into Teddy in the back parking lot? She couldn't imagine the quiet, respectful young man plotting a murder, but if he came face-to-face with a man who his parents had spent potentially thousands of dollars fighting in a lawsuit and nasty words were exchanged, he might have done something on the spur of the moment. She swallowed heavily, uncomfortable at the thought. If he attacked Teddy with the hammer and then realized what he had done and fled, it would explain why he never showed up for his shift that day.

She and Grady spent the rest of the day hacking their way through the brush in the forest. They cleared a path from the back of the yard to the pond, and got started on another path that would wind and curve through the trees to the side yard, coming out near the shed. Flora was confident she would be able to finish the rest of it herself before she had to return the machine. She could hardly believe the progress they had made, and could hardly wait to enjoy the finished result. Amaretto was going to love going for walks through the trees.

They were enjoying some iced lemonade on her porch together when Grady's cell phone rang. She watched as he answered it, and his expression turned to one of shock.

"Yeah, I'll be there in about twenty minutes."

He ended the call, already rising to his feet, and said, "That was Wade. The police are releasing him from custody. I've got to go pick him up."

"Good," she said, her own eyes widening. "That's – that's good, Grady. I'm glad."

She walked him to his truck and kissed him good-bye, watching him go with trepidation. Flora wasn't sure if Wade's release from police custody was a good or bad sign. The lack of evidence against him might mean he was innocent, but she knew there was a lot of red tape when it came to criminal investigations. They very well might be letting a killer go, not because he was innocent, but because they had no way to legally keep him behind bars any longer.

She was worried as she got ready for bed that night. She settled down, tucked into her blankets with Amaretto curled up by her head, listening to the silence of the house around her. The thoughts of Wade reminded her that there were some extremely bad people in this world, and it was at times like these that she keenly felt how isolated she was out there. She had come to love country living, but sometimes, she would rather be back in her apartment, with people all around her. There, at least, if she screamed, someone would be able to hear her.

She woke up to her phone ringing at three in the morning. The transition from sleep to alertness was instant, and the second she saw the time on the clock on her night stand, her stomach dropped. No calls at three in the morning were ever good.

Her dread grew even stronger when she picked up her phone and saw the number on the caller ID. It was the police – not the local police station, but Officer Hendricks's personal work phone. She had saved his number the first time he gave her his card, more than a year ago now.

She didn't want to hear whatever he had to say, but ignoring the call wouldn't make it go away. She answered with shaking fingers. Her mouth suddenly felt dry, and she had to swallow before speaking.

"Hello?"

"Ms. Abner," Officer Hendricks said. "Are you and Grady safe? Neither of you were at the hardware store tonight? No employees there after hours?"

"I'm at home, and as far as I know, Grady is too," she said. "Our employee would not be working at three in the morning. Why? What's going on?"

"There's been a fire," he said grimly.

The fingers of her left hand tightened in the

sheets. "How bad is it?" she asked, her mind racing. They had business insurance, but she didn't know how much of something like this it would cover, or how long it would take for the money to come in if the place had burnt to the ground.

"It's not too bad," he said. "The fire crew has already put out the flames. It's mostly just the front of the store that was damaged – the front counter was the source of the fire, and a window is broken. Someone who lives in one of the nearby apartments came down to take their dog out, and saw the flames. They caught it early. Otherwise, it might have been much worse."

"Oh, thank goodness," she said. "Have you called Grady yet?"

"No." He hesitated. "I know his brother is staying with him. He had to leave the address when he left police custody. I wanted to let you know first. The timing is… suspect."

"What do you mean?" The answer came to her in the next second, before he could respond. "Wait. You think Wade did this? Why would he want to burn down his own brother's business?"

"Why would *anyone* target the hardware store?" Officer Hendricks countered. "You tell me. Do either of you have any enemies out there? People with grudges? People who might think you've been asking too many questions? We've been carrying our own investigation out, Ms. Abner, and we've spoken to some of the same people you have. What you're doing isn't safe."

Her breath caught in her throat. He sometimes warned her away from her amateur sleuthing, but hadn't ever come out and said something as straight-forward as this about it.

"Grady and I have been trying to figure out the truth, and that's all," she said.

"Well, I think it would be wise to take this as a warning," he said. "Until we find the culprit, I suggest you lay low. This fire could just be some teens causing trouble, but I doubt it. I think this is a threat, Flora, and you should take it seriously. No one got hurt this time. Next time, you might not be as lucky."

CHAPTER TWELVE

The fire damage to the hardware store wasn't extensive. It was bad, but it could have been much worse. Or at least, that was what Flora tried to convince herself of as she stared at the mess.

It was the next morning. There was no structural damage, so the firefighters had cleared them to enter the building. Officer Hendricks had met her and Grady there a few minutes ago, and told them there was blatant evidence of an accelerant being used. Between that and the broken window, it was obvious that someone had started the fire intentionally.

The police were looking for the culprit, and they had given Flora and Grady a police report to turn into their insurance. The insurance probably would cover the damage, but it was going to take time to fix, and time to get the store running again.

It wasn't the disaster that it could have been, but it was a setback. Worse, neither of them knew if they might be in further danger. They *had* been snooping around, and even without Officer Hendricks' warning, this would have felt like a warning.

"We'll help you clean," Violet volunteered from where she and Sydney stood together, gazing at the mess.

Violet had seen the damage while she was driving to the coffee shop, and had called Flora in case she didn't know, waking her up just a few hours after she got back to sleep. The five of them – Wade was there too, having apparently insisted on coming with Grady to see the damage that morning – had been looking over the front of the shop somberly. Flora had already called Ellison and left a message on his phone telling him what had happened. As she gazed at the blackened front counter, she had to wonder if he had something to do with this.

It was just a niggling suspicion, between his family's ties to Teddy, and the uncertainty about his schedule on Saturday. The thought made her frown.

"Grady... we kept the schedule on the desk." They kept a paper schedule – with just three of them working there, it hadn't been worth it to upgrade to a computerized program. The schedule was kept on top of the desk or in one of the drawers, along with a lot of their notes, order forms, and receipts.

Grady looked confused for a moment, then his frown deepened, a crease forming between his eyebrows.

"We should have stopped and checked it yesterday," he said.

Flora mentally kicked herself. They really should have. They had discussed the possibility of Ellison being involved, but she didn't think either of them really believed it. She had thought she would just take a glance at the schedule today, when she opened the store, and would see that Saturday was marked as a day off for Ellison after all, then forget about the whole thing. It hadn't felt urgent, just like something she should check and knock off her to-do list when she had the chance.

But now, the schedule was ash. Ellison had said he had a picture of the schedule on his phone, but she hadn't actually seen it. It would be easy for him to pretend that he had deleted the picture, or hadn't taken one after all, and she would have no way to verify anything he said.

Wade was standing a few feet away from them,

his arms crossed, and a puzzled look on his face. "What does that matter?"

Grady shook his head, dismissing the question. "Don't worry about it. We should get a tarp put up over the window," he said. "Wade, will you help?"

"If you need me to stay to help with anything, I can see if one of the other girls can open," Violet said.

"I can let my boss know what happened, I'm sure he'd let me switch shifts with someone," Sydney chimed in.

"No, it's all right," Flora said. "The two of you should get to work."

They had both wanted to see the damage, but Flora didn't want to interrupt their whole day. She asked them for help often enough already.

While Grady and Wade went into the back to get supplies to temporarily patch the window, Flora saw her friends off, promising to call them if there were any updates. After they left, she went back inside and took in the rest of the mess.

While the fire damage had been contained, that wasn't the only thing the arsonist had done. The rest of the store was a mess. Products had been knocked off the shelves, and one of the shelves had even been tipped over. They would have to do inventory, but she would be shocked if some items weren't missing.

Some of the mess came from the firefighters, of course – there was water and muddy footprints all over the floor, but she could hardly blame them for that.

Maybe the likely theft of some of their items was actually a good thing. She held a faint hope that it might help the police catch the culprit. They would be on the lookout for whatever items had been taken once Flora and Grady provided them with a list.

Grady and Wade returned to the front with a stepladder, a large tarp, and the supplies to secure it over the broken window. Wade stepped outside and unfolded the stepladder while Grady took measurements from the inside of the window. Flora watched, not sure if they would need her to help or if she should start cleaning up and taking inventory.

Suddenly, Wade jumped down from the stepladder and muttered a quick, "Stay there, I'll be right back," as he jogged off down the sidewalk. Slowly, Grady lowered the tape measure and stared after his brother.

"He's always done this," he said with a sigh. "I thought he'd be more help." He paused. "Just so you know, I don't think he started the fire – we were both raised to believe that family sticks together no matter what, and I don't think he would want to sabotage me like this. But I'm coming to realize I might not have known who he really is for a long time."

"Did he seem to act suspiciously at all when the two of you arrived?" Flora asked quietly.

He shook his head. "He seemed just as shocked and angry as I was expecting. Though he wouldn't get out of the truck until after Officer Hendricks left."

"I guess we aren't certain that the killer and the arsonist are the same person, but it's probably safe to assume the two things are connected." She gave him a weak smile and a hopeful look. "So, if Wade didn't have anything to do with this, then maybe he didn't have anything to do with Teddy's death, either."

Grady nodded, looking a little more positive. Before either of them could say anything else, someone came running up to the store, only to backpedal as they passed the broken window. Flora looked up to see Ellison poking his head through the hole.

"I need your help!" he said. "Some guy just attacked another guy down the street. It looks bad."

CHAPTER THIRTEEN

Grady ran toward the door and Flora followed him, turning down the sidewalk in the direction Ellison pointed them toward – the same direction they had seen Wade go. She heard Ellison running after them, just a few feet behind her.

"Around the corner, there," he said, gesturing to an alley when she glanced back at him.

Grady turned the corner a few steps ahead of Flora. Slowing, she hesitated. Was this a trap? All of the strange coincidences surrounding Ellison came to the forefront of her mind, and she stumbled a little as she faltered, but Grady was already in the alley and she didn't want to let him go alone, so she followed him with Ellison right behind her.

She stumbled to a stop when she saw Wade

pinning a man against the alley wall. It took her a second to recognize Zeke. He had a bloody nose, and looked terrified.

"Wade," Grady snapped. "What are you doing? Let him go."

"Nah, I don't think I will," Wade muttered. "No one messes with my family."

Beside Flora, Ellison panted, clutching a stitch in his side. "What is going on? Do you know this guy?"

"He's Grady's brother," she said. "Did you see what happened?"

He nodded. "I was walking over to see the damage to the store, when I saw him punch the other guy and drag him into the alley. It was crazy, I've never seen anything like that. I was looking for help, which is when I saw you guys in the store. Is he crazy or something?"

Wade must have heard him, because he looked over with a glare. "I ain't crazy. I'm doing this to protect my brother."

"What are you talking about?" Grady asked. Zeke opened his mouth as if he was about to say something, but Wade shot him a dark look and he closed it again.

"I've been thinking about everything that happened," Wade said. "I had a lot of time to do nothing *but* think while I was in the holding cell. Some things weren't lining up for me. When I saw Zeke walking down the road, I knew I had to talk to him." His glare at the other man intensified. "You want to know what he said? He said, 'Now that I took care of Teddy, we can pick up where we left off with the scrap business. Just tell your brother stop snooping around, will you?'"

Flora gasped. Grady looked surprised, then angry, while Ellison just looked confused.

"I have no idea what's going on. Should I call the police or not?"

Flora jerked her head down in a nod. "Please do. Tell them to hurry."

He fumbled as he pulled his phone out of his pocket, his hands shaking. "Who's getting in trouble? Your brother or that other guy?"

"The other guy's name is Zeke Jefferson," Flora said. "And… I think he's the one who killed Teddy Martin. And probably set the store on fire, too."

Zeke started struggling in Wade's grip. "Let me go, man. I thought you'd be *happy*. Teddy was the one who framed you all those years ago and got you put in prison, and he's the reason our business failed and my life fell apart. He was the one behind everything bad that's happened to us over the past five years. When he ran me down and acted like a hero after I tried to shoplift, I just snapped. Went around to the back of the store, grabbed a hammer out of the bed of his truck, waited for him to come out, and got him good with it when he wasn't looking. Do you think he didn't deserve what I did to him?"

"Sure, he might've deserved it," Wade said easily. Flora winced. Wade might not have killed anyone, but that didn't necessarily mean he was a good guy. "But you killed him on property my brother owns, and *I* got pinched for it. Then you set my brother's store on fire. I know you did, don't try and lie. You don't mess with my family, Zeke. You should have known better."

"The fire was just to send a message," Zeke said. "A warning. I wouldn't have hurt Grady, I just wanted him to stop snooping around. They came by my house and questioned me, did you know that? Trying to figure out what happened, track down the real killer because they didn't believe it was you."

"I'm touched," Wade said, grinning over at Grady and Flora. "But it doesn't change the fact that you messed up, Zeke. Now, because I am a changed man who is trying to make something of his life, I'm not going to hurt you unless you try to run away. We're going to wait right here, and you'll tell the police everything." He frowned. "I'd appreciate it if, for the sake of our friendship, you'd tell them about what happened all those years ago, when Teddy planted those drugs in my car. I should've known you weren't my real friend when you never showed up to testify on my behalf."

"The – the police are on their way," Ellison chimed in. He looked terrified. "This is… um, a lot. I did *not* expect all of this when you two hired me."

Flora felt a sudden pang of guilt as she looked at Ellison where he stood, pale and shaking. How could she possibly have suspected *him* of being the killer?

Zeke struggled trying to wrench out of Wade's grip, but Grady moved forward to help restrain him. Flora watched as the two brothers kept a firm hold on Wade's old friend.

They had caught the killer, but she still wished they could have done more. Teddy Martin might have been flawed and a criminal in his own right, but he hadn't deserved to die in the hardware store's parking lot. Now, he would never be able to answer for his role in framing Wade and taking away years of his life in prison.

EPILOGUE

It took them a week to finish cleaning the hardware store, take inventory, and replace everything that was damaged. With the new front counter, new computer, fresh paint, and new window, the store looked better than it had before the fire, which was a small consolation for the two of them.

Oddly, Flora had never seen the place so busy. It seemed like everyone in town wanted to stop in and ask them about what happened. She was a little surprised that Ellison decided to keep working for them. She was glad, though – he was finally relaxing around them a little bit, and seemed like he would be a good, reliable employee for a long time… though, she wouldn't blame him for leaving if something like Teddy's death and the arson happened again.

Wade was still staying with Grady, but he was already making some money of his own. The scrap business Teddy Martin owned wasn't going to reopen; she had seen the post on Warbler's social media page a few days ago. Wade had jumped in to fill the niche even before the announcement was posted.

For now, he was borrowing Grady's truck to haul scrap metal to a salvage yard a few towns over, for a low fee to his clients, but he was already talking about making it into a real business. She didn't think she trusted Wade yet, and didn't know if she would *ever* completely trust him, but he did seem to be trying. For Grady's sake, she was glad that he was around.

Slowly, life returned to normal, as it always seemed to do. She finished cutting the paths through the trees behind her house, and the new tiles for her bathroom floors came in on the first delivery truck they got at the hardware store after the fire. She left them sitting in the foyer at her house for the time being. Things were still busier than normal at the hardware store, and most of her focus was there.

Still, in the back of her mind, she felt a clock ticking down. She had just under a year left at the house now. A year to finish all of the projects on her list and deal with anything unexpected that came up.

A year before she would either have to find

another house to flip in the area, or say goodbye to all of her friends and her life here and move on.

Warbler was a town where time ran slowly and the summer days seemed to last forever, but her own clock seemed to be moving faster and faster. One day soon, she was going to have to decide if she had it in her to move on from Warbler and her friends here, or if she needed to rethink her career in house flipping.

Printed in Great Britain
by Amazon